Salt Works
P O E M S

Michael Chitwood

Michael Chitwood

Ohio Review Books • Athens, Ohio

Salt Works

Copyright © 1992 Michael Chitwood
All rights reserved

Design: Joyce Barlow Dodd
Composition: Sans Serif

Acknowledgments and thanks are made to the editors of the following
magazines in which these poems first appeared:

Antioch Review (Real Jazz)
Blue Pitcher (Big House)
Fine Madness (The Hardened Arm)
Mississippi Review (Grease)
Malahat Review (Shenandoah Valley Triptych, Seeing the Lights)
The Ohio Review (Transport, I'll Fly Away, History of the Country, Talking to Patsy Cline,
Dust, Wednesday Blues, Juke)
Poetry East (When Country People Come In, Weave Room)
River City (Martyrdom of the Onions)
Southern Humanities Review (Thinking of Rome in Fair Lea, West Virginia)
Southern Poetry Review (Leaving Saltville, Signs, Hard Surface Road, Dogwood)
Threepenny Review (The Story as Told by Ice, The Mill, Leaving Town, Appetite)
Virginia Quarterly Review (Photographs from the Mountain Empire)
Zone 3 (Charon at the Esso)

Some of the poems also appeared in the chapbook, *Martyrdom of the Onions*, Nightshade Press, Troy, Maine. "The Mill" and "Leaving Town" appeared in the anthology *A Song for Occupations*, Wayland Press, Denver, Colorado.

The author is grateful to the North Carolina Arts Council for a grant that helped with the completion
of this book and to Tom Andrews, Michael McFee, Eileen Gordy, and Wayne Dodd
for hacking through the underbrush.

Library of Congress Cataloging in Publication Data
Chitwood, Michael
    Salt Works : poems / Michael Chitwood.
    p. cm.

(An Ohio Review Book)

I. Title.

PS3553.H535S24   1992
811'.54—dc20   92-27430
                                                            CIP

ISBN 0-942148-15-0
ISBN 0-942148-14-2

For Jean, the flavoring

Transport

You can wake up in Rome
and go to sleep in War, West Virginia. *
You can be so moved
that the strobe of the only caution light
on the empty streets of 3 a.m. War
throbs the same as your heart, your head
still awake in the old light of Rome.
What of it,
people fly everyday.
No need to be amazed
the way these hillbillies were,
leaving town on the "Brother Johnson,"
or "Friend of Charleston,"
for the glide down to Richmond
where you could buy bananas anytime
and the lights stayed on all night.

* S. of Charleston W Va., just above Va. border

Leaving Saltville ✱

One of these days I'm going to cut and go.
Crossing the field,
will I look over the right shoulder
or the left

to the old story?
By the Holsten River, the men started in a field
but went underneath
for what would keep the meat
on the long march.
At night, the hands still held shovels,
arms worked, eyes moved.
Such chambers the sweat-stained broadcloth discovered.
The ear below the sweatband could hear the sea,
beneath the broomstraw and quartz, a shore.

There's a worn place in the field,
a depression
like the one in the palm,
where animals come to lick the ground.

When you leave town,
the field is your only address.
It speaks your name,
takes care of your ride,
offers you a salary,
a dream, a crystal like ice.
It knows what we don't know we know.
It remembers us.

The ones who stay behind will eat their daily portion.
The deer will carry us into the woods.

✱ W. of Marion, N of I 81

The Story as Told by Ice

At the Raphine Sav-A-Lot   See p. 40
we put them in the back,
shut the camper shell,
each with his favorite sleeping bag
to sleep the rest of the way.

*

The cold limbs
of hardwoods held long sentences of snow,
sentences being repeated
like the prayer of someone who doesn't believe
what has happened.
The sky was darker than the ground.

*

How far did you travel?
How many times did you look over your shoulder?
Did you notice the left hand glove still on the dash?
Did you hear breathing?
Anything that sounded like breathing?
Did you hold the empty hand?

*

We followed our lights,
twin sticks to see by.
Like the blind, we could see
only as far as the lights
reached into the dark.

*

When we came to the end and home,
turning down the last and only road
that would bring us to where
we wanted to be,
the two were still warm,
peaceful in our monoxide.

*

Solstice and too cold for salt to work
on the empty road.
The snow plow light
throbs on the wall,
caution, dark, caution, dark.
The ground shines.
In the morning, everything will be closed.

I'll Fly Away

There's a snag in the oak.
A dust of snow reveals the harvest stubble
as lines on a page
and they are only rows of harvest stubble.
There's the red fruit of the holly
and the cedar's blue.
There's the glitter of the moon on ice
and it's only glitter.
There's a snag in the oak
I can't get by.

*

Rodney said he wouldn't go.
I said I wouldn't.
Wendell said he would and was gone
from the back pew
to where the reformed Hindu, now evangelist, wept
because his mother and father died
Hindu and he would never see them
on the Shores of Glory.
I went.

*

Can God make a door so small
he can't get through it?
Can he do anything?
There was only the moon
in its cold path, straight and narrow.

*

Beggar's-lice on my knees keep asking for the field.
I believe what they believe.
I believe in the thistle at the right hand,
the mortal rip,
the salt of the body.

Yes

For three days, we have to take it with us,
like hauling around a chest freezer.
We have to make arrangements for it.
We have to make allowances for it.
Where will it sit?
Are the doors large enough to bring it in?
Can we back the car close enough?
Can you ever get close enough?
It takes six to carry it.
One person can guide it
once the spindly legs are down.
They break and fold under for loading.
At first, I'm afraid
it will collapse somewhere,
snagged in pile carpeting.
You can see exactly where it's been
like tire tracks in soft ground.
The first night we almost forgot.
Everyone was getting their coat,
saying where we would meet the next day.
Then we remembered
and had to run out to the parking lot
to round up some help.
Once it lodged in a hallway,
some people on one side, some on the other.
On the third day, I set a drink on it
to receive a hug.
I wiped it immediately, the glossy walnut so beautiful.
We had shopped for hours among the choices.
We made the right decision, don't you think?
Yes, I think we did.

History of the Country

In the early years, her parents lived in Roanoke, which in some Indian tongue means Big Lick. It was called that because the soil there was high in salt, and animals came out of the woods to lick the ground.

They worked at a textile factory everyone called "The Silk Mill." Afternoons after work, they played croquet in a park until they couldn't see.

So, what we expected I don't know. After work it was so hot we slept and sweated. Her little scissors kicks sent us gliding in the currents. Such journeys—movement on a river with long stretches of slow, almost still water. Our long boats nudged the plumage of flocks of swans that were unafraid. Bats scooped plump mosquitoes from the dusk over pools. Rafts of live vegetation sailed, sometimes with a cargo of cottonmouths and opossum. In a similar fashion, Jefferson brought fluted designs up the Rivanna.

Appetite

The frenzied wriggling
of maggots
is a sexual ecstasy,
the happiness of their bodies
which is the happiness
of the working mouth.
Over lunch,
I heard a woman
say to another,
"And your sexual appetite?"
Appetite being the cry
we are born with
and come to explain
in talk, talk being
an evolved eating,
a hunger
to mouth the unknowable
like a child
with a small, smooth rock.

My good aunts first worried
and whispered to each other
when he stopped eating.
"Not a bite," they'd say
coming down the hall.
And later
we came back to a house
neighbors had filled
with fried chicken,
tomatoes, sweet potatoes,
even warm blackberry cobbler.

Talking To Patsy Cline

"Crazy"

Me with a steady job
and the post office won't take a check
I have to talk to the man
through a hole in the glass.

I do interviews for a living,
phone surveyor,
I say to the man's lips.
His hands dart out under the glass,
snake heads
seeing if the hawk is out.

He's not listening.
Hands are deaf and spade-head as a cottonmouth.
I wave at the hole in the glass.

For the interviews,
I have to get Momma's smokehouse
and back-door trot
out of my voice.
I can do it too.
People think they're talking to someone
from Show-Me or Buckeye.

Where are you,
people sometimes ask?
I say it doesn't matter,
Sir or Ma'am.
If we could continue.

We all have our three walls.
I've got Patsy Cline pinned up
and hum "Crazy"

before someone answers.
No one has caught me yet.

I ask a lot.
Age? Race? Marital status?
How many times per week
do you go to the grocery store?
Are you more likely to go
in the morning or evening?

We don't get to ask why.
That's the only one.
Sometimes I say it in my head
after everything they say.
Why? Why? Why?
Like a kid that's just found the word.

Would you marry a man with one leg?
Would you let a snake on you?
Do you think God knows
about the back of the bus?
Well, what do you say?
I ask them in my head.
They don't know me or the questions
I don't ask.

Some questions come out of the blue.
Are there multiple births in your family?
Have you ever traveled outside the country?
Where? How long did you stay?
Given the chance,
would you go back?

We aren't supposed to show a preference.
A preference will get you fired.
I don't show anything,
I just ask.

The post office man won't come out
from behind his frosted glass.
These have to go I say.
They're ends that have to be tied.
He won't take a check.
I go outside with my handful.
Now, I'm thinking, now
I've got to go home with these.

"I Fall to Pieces"

The day Patsy Cline died
in an airplane crash
"I Fall to Pieces" was number one
on the charts.

That's what I was thinking
when the woman picked up
and said, "Can't talk;
I'm alt'a pieces."
I heard the screen-door slap
in her voice.
She was from somewhere
I grew up.

It spooked me.
I had to go out to the picnic table
and take deep breaths.

Patsy's poster is a black and white,
which I guess was all they had,
but they've colored it.
Gave her a red hat
and rouged her cheeks.

She looks like a corpse, Melinda says.
But she's on my side.
When a woman answers,
I look up and talk to Patsy.

We don't get to pick out numbers.
The computer dials
and when we hang up,
it goes on.

So, I couldn't call back
to see if I could help.
I'd offer to keep her kids
or bring over something
or we could go drink beer
and play Ernest Tubb.

We wear headsets,
so the person answers
inside your head.
All day people say "Hello."
Sometimes, they pick up
before it rings.
Then we're waiting
like we're going to hear a secret.

At home, I've dialed Momma's number,
and after the recording
about the number being disconnected
I listen to the hum
like it's a coincidence —
we picked up at the same time
and in a second she'll say "Hello?"

"Faded Love"

Momma talked to Patsy Cline one time.
Patsy was doing an interview
on a call-in radio show,
and you could ask her anything.

Patsy was talking to people
like they were kin.

All of a sudden
there was Momma with Patsy
in the green plastic box
on the kitchen cabinet.

"If the only way people could see you
was by your voice,
what would you look like?"
That took Patsy a minute.
It got quiet.
You could hear her breathe.
"Trouble and honey," she said.
"Trouble and honey."

Momma wouldn't look at the picture
they printed in the paper when she died.
"I know what Patsy looks like," she said.

I told that story
at the picnic table during lunch.
"You OK?" Melinda asked me
right in front of everybody.
"It takes a year or two to get over," she said.
Melinda watches too many talk shows.

On the way to work
I saw a guy talking on the phone in his car.
I started wondering if we ever get them.
That would be a hoot.
He don't know where we are.
We don't know where he is.
Everybody's talking out of nowhere.

Signs

"Once the sign comes
you can't get shed of it,"
my grandmother said,
using the dying verb.
She meant three owl screeches
three nights in a row
or a single star
inside a circle around the moon
on the birthday of an aged friend.

"It's hurt," someone guessed.
But what it meant
none of the neighbors could say
when a buzzard perched
on a streetlight in the subdivision.
We were too far from the country
of our memories.
All I know
is the lamp's sensor
read darkness
under those black feathers,
and the light began to come on.

II

Dust

1
God said to Jacob
I shall make your descendants like the dust of the earth.
It was just like the Lord,
always the twin meaning.

2
Like us, dust clings to the what-nots.
Like dust, we find our place among the stones and grass blades.
Our history is a history
of rise and fall.

3
From the beginning,
  we were dust got up,
dust got up in helmet and mail.
  Truly, it loves us as a brother.
Wise, it has settled our squabbles for centuries
  with its fine logic.

4
A man travels from the place of his birth.
Dust is the road
and the contents of his pockets,
the coin of the land he will spend to enter,
brushing off his sleeves.

5
We are descendants of dust
  and I am happy when I see it rise
in shafts of light,
  Solomon in the temple at dawn,
climbing the east stairs.

Hard Surface Road

That summer they took off a corner of the cemetery. I watched from behind the stone where the lamb folded its forelegs in marble. The men drank water from Mason jars they asked me to fill. A brass basket spilled its roses on a stone rolled like a settee cushion and dented where someone slept: "Gone but not forgotten." The men shaved the graveyard bank. "The crooked shall be made straight," one said, handing back the jar smeared with his finger dirt. I rode the gate of the Perdue plot, raising the latch and going in slow. It took all of June for them to make the turn and go down the Thurman road. The dust followed every truck and powdered the stones like talc. I could go only as far as the graveyard, and they piled the jars like rocks, the mouths open in all directions. They chimed and shifted when I picked one up. When the crew moved out of sight, the dust was settled and would fly no more.

Thinking of Rome in Fair Lea, West Virginia

Help me remember,
I wanted to say to the man wrestling the drag chain
onto the back of the fair's largest John Deere,
what is the name of the church that holds
St. Peter's bones and a bit of the chain
in which he was brought to Rome.
This thing could drag a whale from the deep
if you could find a way to hook him up, he said.
Of the man shouting about elephant rides, tigers and the rare black
    leopard,
I wanted to ask what entrance
the emperors used to process into the coliseum
and how many gates sorted the people of Rome into their seats.
You will see amazing feats, he said:
men consumed in flame and yet not burned.
The man with the "Kill'em All Let God Sort'em Out" tee shirt
said nothing but pulled the lever
and set the neon bones of the Ferris wheel whirling,
rattling above the souls along the midway
like link chain jangling on the ankles of the vanquished.

*The Great Wheeled Words from
the Terminal Dispatcher*

They groan and clog
Blackwater hill, jockeying
with their remaining momentum.
OneWay, ThruHaul, TrueLine, Overnite,
they reach for a lower gear
and we follow.
On the other side, they flash their lights
if you are in the way of their hurling.

*

Slow like alcohol in the blood,
one works through the streets
of a small town.
The wide turn
nicks the five and dime.
It lodges in an intersection,
and all
of Saturday night backs up behind.

*

Broke down on I-40
its wherewithal scattered
around its hood,
which is tipped like a hat,
one of them seems both
tired and civil
as we take ourselves home
by its stalled adverb.

*

Here's one, its paranoia
stuck like a tick to its back.
How's my driving? Please call.

*

*An insult
to the thoracic cavity,*
like the impact of a name called.
It was actually
the pearl of speed,
the insect-sized tablet
that pushed its soft snout
into the narrows
of his wrist and ankle
and put in
and took out
in equal measure.

*

The word he lived by,
that had followed him
all his days and nights
in caffeine booths
and toll gates,
that could take up all the spaces
of a convenience store,
that could block out the sun
for the passerby,
drove him onto the wheel.
Oiled with years of his touch,
the wheel held him to his word.

*

Loaded with someone's life savings
on a cross country gamble,
they cough and open their eyes.
You can feel them idling
in your shoes as you approach,
feel them burning their fossils
in the terminal's asphalt lot.
Greased and satiated, they lumber
into the slow, inscrutable sentences,
hauling who knows what,
antennae, reflective paint, jumpsuits,
salt to open snow-clogged roads?

Charon at the Esso

The gears of his walk
are missing some teeth.
Every five steps
he stops and waits
for the chains and sprockets
to catch.
It's the space
that comes into life
with use
like the arthritic hand
of the grandfather
clock, stalling in mid-jump
from minute to minute
until the slack plays out
and time goes on.
It's the half seconds
you never get over,
like the message
on his wrecker,
"Twenty-three and a Half
Hour Service."
Where are those bad thirty minutes?

His alligator died
and two weeks the tank idled
beside the nab rack,
with only the cloudy water
and putrid rafts of hamburger.
He had it stuffed for its smile
and draped over the cash register.
"One million years of cold blood
and this one stops ticking
over meat gone sour."
The law keeps them wild

for just that reason
to enjoy what comes into the water
pink and struggling.

He gave me my first
brassy kiss of beer
and keeps them cold
in the humming, red coffin
that says "Coke" in the corner.
Half an hour everyday,
he won't get you out
of the sumac and chokecherry,
car flipped, the minute hands
of the flattened Johnson grass
slowly coming back up
toward the pale hour.

Winter Coming

On the back porch
the wind slams the screen door coming in.
The first time I learned the lesson of the seasons
was a Saturday morning in 1964, in my miniature rocker,
my father coming in with red eyes, my uncle with him
because my grandfather died in the night.
The sparrow cheeps in his tree.
The fence gate bats the post.
For every winter there is something pinned on the coat
like my name and bus number
the day I went to first grade
and not to the funeral.
The empty clothesline bows out the way the wind blows.
The crow is knocked sideways.
The wood stove sucks its teeth
and the elm sings in the fire.
The sway of old electric lines
makes the lamplight billow and fade.

Shenandoah Valley Triptych

From the County

There was one run, he said, out past the Honey Hole and then up the valley to New Market, that the engineer liked to make at night. Somewhere in the country, it was too dark to tell exactly where, the engineer would give two hoots on the whistle, and a light in a farmhouse blinked back. Word was the engineer had a redhead there.

The winking made him think of the spring electricity came to the county. The crew that strung cables by the house whistled at his mother hanging out clothes. Bees worried the pear tree and followed the blooms down. Her skirts and sheets lifted on the line. Above the rails later, current hummed and went the way the men disappeared, into drugstores and county offices.

He left and went to work for the N&W, and his parents added a porch and livingroom. The face of the house turned from the tracks toward the new road to town. The engineer always punched his arm and nodded when they went by the place. It made him a little mad, as if the engineer knew something about the place he didn't.

Visiting, he still watched the back and the engines pulling their sentences of freight and flat cars across the pastures. He read Soo Line, Soo Line, blank, Ohio, blank, Chesapeake, Chesapeake and understood. Mornings, coming into a town on top of his chosen word, he could see women still in their nightclothes.

Tryst

The train came closer, moaned, then moaned again.
"Why did you do that?" he asked.
"Sorry it was an accident."
"Twice?"

He was in early. Usually he would still be dumping silage on the horned heads pushing under the lantern light. He had not wanted electricity in the barn. "Never work for a man with lights in his barn, you'll work all night," he said when they hooked up the house.

The table dampened under its oilcloth. Little bouquets in the linoleum had disappeared under blushes of mud.

"This place needs a breeze," she said and slid up the pane. The curtains, her skirts, moved on what came in. The night's engine, pulling its accounted cargo in sparks and abandon, faded toward New Market and was overcome by the shrill of tree frogs.

A late traveller, passing the humped rows of the new-turned garden, could see them through the screen, him concentrating on fork and knife, her, hand on the jamb, just realizing it was the dark that winked to the train.

Shenandoah

    Three, sometimes four, times each week, he took his loaded, coupled words up the valley. He loved the oiled spaces between, four feet of jump and still air. The country blurred and fed into speed.

    Raw lumber, stacked on the flat cars, set a scaffold on the breeze, and they brought houses to rest by the Shenandoah, James, and Blackwater. Yards of undyed cloth, banded for the dyer, were hauled on and the doors made the words whole again.

    That spring, at a switchyard where the late trains were made up, he watched the bees frenzy spinster wisteria. They lowered themselves over the purple lace on humming wires and let themselves down petal to petal heavy with pollen.

    Speed was in the engineer's wrist. "This is where I live," he said, pointing at the needle trembling on sixty. When the cars swayed and shook their doors as though the words would open, the engineer would say to him, "Are you going to jump?"

    "I'll go when you go," he said. Sometimes they would ride miles into the valley without speaking.

Martyrdom of the Onions

In a garden, they are knots along a rope of dirt.
Pulled out and hung in a bundle on the back porch,
they chime in deep tones against the wood frame.
I have seen my father rub a half on the lintel
of a rabbit trap, to erase the smell of his hands.
Lines of longitude describe their globe;
in cities on the other side
you would live a few hours over again.
They fit the palm like a door knob.
Open one and put your tongue on the core;
it will fasten to you like dry ice.
In their parchments are the records
of the temples and the loaded barges
and the number of souls and their whereabouts.
In a dark closet,
their hearts germinate
and drive green spikes through the bodies.

Photographs from the Mountain Empire

They collect in the shade of pin-oaks,
Sunday, after lunch, coats off,

sleeves rolled and chairs,
brought into the yard, tipped back.

The ones who can name them all
are dead or gone in memory

and the time hasn't come when you smile
at unknown devices

so they rest and look from the shade.

*

Cane-back, snake and rider, double stitch.
Pie safe, swing blade, chain trace.

Tail and squeal were all they wasted.
Peach halves glowed like lantern wicks

in the dirt-walled cellar.

Far down in December
you could sicken on those banked sugars.

*

They birthed each other,
cut teeth on each other,

picked up pieces the saw dropped
to keep them from the dogs.

They damned each other,
smeared the same jar

with finger dirt.

They shaved a deal,
came to blows, shots

and all the women gathered
to wash the body.

*

Lard smoked for reading John.

Tick, chigger, and poison oak
smouldered along the beltline.

Split oak seasoned in ricks.
Pine gummed the chimney.

Farther up the mountain
cousin sparked cousin

*

"You didn't miss what you didn't know."
But town came out.

Kids got afraid of the dark.
Clear-cut, chestnut oak was left

to rot to make a path
for those drooping ropes

of electricity.

*

After Revelations, scratched
on a few blank pages,

the known generations.
Sparrel T. and Governor,

who held no office,
is as far back as anyone

thought to write down.

*

At the annual gathering,
she reigns over potluck

from her webbed lawn chair,
one hundred and three frail

pounds, from which
this crowd fell.

*

"Smack a fart out of you that hums like a jarfly,"
my uncle said when I corrected his English.

Spring apple bough or witch hazel,
the booted group couldn't agree

but well-rig, dump trucks and back hoe
waited until the rattling pick-up arrived.

He got it from his grandfather,
followed the wand around the site

then said, "Here, drill here."

*

Hogs do headstands,
joyous in rendering.

Grandma, aunts,
unmarried uncles reach in,

smiling for the new camera.

The hogs are dressed,
and one sports a fly

on the white meat
like a beauty mark.

Big House

Leaves hurry in the yard.
The Johnson grass sways, the sumac and thistle,
the stem in the seed still on the stem.

Wind is the road out of here.
Wind is the color of what it goes around.
It repeats itself.

What bothers you, bothers you.
The thing you don't see
puts the tear in your eye.

The wind is a big house.
You can lean on it.
It's where you hang your hat.

Wind says what there is to say.
Curtains worry at the window.
The wind thumbs a page.

It will slam your doors
and rattle the what-nots.
The heavy-headed grass nods.

You can believe in the wind.
It tastes like praying,
like paper, like a moth wing, like breathing.

Dogwood

Because the tilt of the earth
                             and the rotation
at this time of day and year
soaks the antique doilies of the blooming dogwood
with a light like blood,
                       I have forgotten how old I am
and can only arrive
at the proper figure
                 by subtracting from the present.

*

It is the color of blood collected
in the cellophane that wraps meat,
                             the pools gathered
in many folds, like a rose,
                     underneath the styrofoam tray,
the slow issue,
as the meat becomes room temperature.

*

Right now, the radio is saying
                        we're going to hear
about vast, underground river systems,
if we stay tuned.
             I think the dogwood sprays are antenna dishes,
they are receiving something in the coming dark.

*

In our age, it is possible
                 to read the heart's correspondence
with its far-flung empire.

In our age, it is possible to chill the body,
                                      hold the living heart in your hand
and then give it back to its beating.
In the reverse light of the angiogram,
                            our circulation
is cloudy and drifting like smoke.
It goes its own way, forked and random
                                   like the stunted dogwood branches,
cursed for their part in Salvation.

               *

God damned the dogwood
                        and stained its blossom
at the four points of the white compass
for holding his son while he died.
Blood now in every direction,
                        blood at the horizon
of every petal.

               *

Because its limbs were so low,
                        it was the first tree
I could climb, although now I can't say
how old I was when I fell
and received my first scar.

               *

It becomes the understory of the long-leafed pine,
                                          the scrimshaw,
the tusk, the bone, the baleen lyre
that hangs in the shade of the taller trees.

               *

I remember now
               how far I am from birth,
how odd it is to wake to the hum of tires on interstate,
the blossoms losing color, blanching like the nausea
when you see the smile
               of the wound, your blood spurting
to the rhythm of your hard-working, imbecile heart,
beating itself to death.

Seeing the Lights

When I see the lights
at White's Truckstop, off Interstate 81,
I think of people I love

the electric hum in chill air
incandescent tubes, buzzing
with their best line,
their one line, light.

In the parking lot,
there is the faint country music of the place
and the big words idling,
Thruhaul, Trueline, Oneway,
words that lumber through the streets of small towns.

When I see the lights, unaccountably,
I think of people I love,
then the words, coming to Raphine,* Steeles Tavern **
and out again across the illiterate fields.

*W of I-81, SW of Staunton
** E. of I-81 at that point

III

The Hardened Arm

What he wants he can't say. Seven o'clock and the hill back lit. The dusk closes the throats of the four o'clocks. The day's grease and smear accounts along his pant's leg. Gear-nicked, his arm escaped the teeth again, but not the time of day. Dew martyrs on the grass blades. Morning glories turn the locks on their plush lounges. Bumblebees stumble home. He tightens his grip on the arm of the lawn chair, checks for a pulse in its curved wrist. What he wants. . . the dirt road ribbons in the faint light. . . he wants to have at his fingertips like the point of the pocketknife, above the quick, above the half moons.

When Country People Come In

When country people come in
to work at the Silk Mill,
their name for it,
they bring whole tomatoes
in their brown sacks.
On the squat stool
where they take breaks,
they open those Early Girls
and Better Boys,
big as a heart,
and the red pulp runs
to their elbows.

When country people come in
you can see them singing
though you can't hear
over the loom-thrash.
They mouth "Jesus,"
the pucker and the smile
like a kiss,
the savior on their lips.

When country people come in
they come to be of use
because they have taken off a belt
to splice a harness
and they've emptied feed sacks
to hem and fill
with Sunday-school children
and of use
is the only way to trick
a living from the dirt.

The Mill

Late afternoon, some coolness comes to the seared grass.
The thrush stitches in his one note,
pushed and drawn through the still, humid air.
I can't say why another afternoon,
the weaver bent over the day's breakdown,
attaches to this one.

Somebody with a bolt of cloth hit the lever.
The machine grabbed the strands
of the shoulder-length hair.

It was the blank of the afternoon;
someone making the usual pitch and swing
to shoulder a bolt and haul it
to the cloth room
where the nine ladies read
each undyed bolt for defect.
They unspool the long white pages
and memorize the lesson there.
It was just the droning of the afternoon,
thinking how Goldsboro and Cherew and Rocky Mount* and Ferrum*
   are shot into space,
the capsule later swaying back to splashdown on parachutes of local
   weave;
maybe thinking how New York makes a cloth deal with the Japanese
or how Hank Williams and John Wesley work here
and when the squat, slope-shouldered man with the baseball-size chew
squalls in Kawliga,
it will be Friday and another week done,
another week done.

This afternoon's machine has you.
Put your ear to the warp, the loom page,
listen to its hum.

Today, the steel-tipped shuttle could have sewn your eyes shut.
Swaddling clothes, sheet or suit to be laid out in,
what have you made?
As you drift away, flat on your back, someone mouths your name
and you keep going.

This is a narrow path, 44 inches wide.
This is the cloth path they will sometime roll up and cart off.
Fixer, Weaver, Cloth Doffer, you will be lucky to go until you can go
    no farther.

When he came back to work,
black thread held the lips of his wound together.
In the weave room he nodded to the people he met.
The tiny pink mouth smiled at everyone.

I'm remembering quitting time, how they filed out
through a narrow door.
They picked the filaments from their clothes,
and let them go
to thread into the thousand eyelets of the late afternoon.

Leaving Town

In the last light of this afternoon,
the rails glaze and seem to lift.
In the light of this afternoon,
the bare maple branches and the poplar
lift up their arms.
They praise the loaded freight cars in the station.
They praise the groan and sigh of air-brakes releasing,
as the train, heavy with uncolored cloth, pulls away.
This afternoon's engine strains, throttles up out of its morning stall.
The cloth train, loaded with hundreds of hours of work,
the blank yards of the bolts,
the cardboard boxes of afternoons spun out, banded with metal straps,
  moves.
If you could detach one hour from the long, coupled train,
would it matter which one?
Would it be a certain time of day
when steel rails and pitch-coated crossties
become a Jacob's Ladder out of town,
rising up to the darkening blue between clay banks?
Would it be the time you're tired
and lie down to rest a while?

Pocket Shield

This was work,
the white, plastic sheath
he put in every morning,
last thing in front of the mirror.

Quiver of signatures,
what did all those colors mean?
And the tiny ruler,
had he ever used its wooden half foot?
We had desires
on that full sleeve,
the exotic hues of his occupation.
We put them to work in flowers, stick people.
Some evenings we could take out
the pen-shaped flashlight,
a gift from the Draper Corporation,
"Makers of Quality Looms."
We got our turn at doctor,
peering into his mouth
and down the red passageways of his ears.
We did not see, those nights,
the tally marks each day struck.
The shield with its "Safety First" slogan
kept them hidden.

Reed Hooks

They look like the levers
that '70s guitarists worked
to get that torn screech
that caused these people
to say to their children
"Is that what you call music?"
Each one has his own
reed hook, the handle
a blue metallic glitter
or red lava-lamp swirl
though some are covered
with masking tape and dirt-
stained from their fingers,
and they reach through
to the strings of the warp
and pull the wayward
yarn back to tie
and they throw the switch
on the loom to start it
and its deafening music.

Weave Room

Because the room roared,
two hundred Draper looms
throttled to make the most
of extra-yard bonus,
and because they made
the machines sing until
they carried deafness
home like an empty
lunch box,
they mastered a speech
held in hands.
I've seen fights begin
from the way one
took hold of another
to move him away
from a breakdown.
Gossip traveled
on fingertips.
But best of all
was the semaphore
they invented
with the flashlights
they used to understand
the greased hearts of looms.
Hanging in thongs,
voices potent as the rock
in David's sling.
They spoke across
the scream of the room,
shot the air
with syllables of light.

Lunch Bags

Small, brown, worn
by carrying
almost to a cloth.

In the morning
they bulge
with whole, fat tomatoes,
hard tupperware squares
for mayonnaised bread.

After lunch,
I see them fold down
like private letters
and put in back pockets,

the emptiness
to be used again.

Wednesday Blues

Days like this
I'd like to blow big folding money,
waste enough presidents to leave America
leaderless well into the next century.

I'm talking hard-earned money on easy living
so that I'd be sorry of it
or called sorry for doing it.

Days like this
I consider all the days I've hung
by the knot of a necktie,
all the small-time criminal days
hauled in on a misdemeanor
and swung on a paisley noose,
and everyone ratted on a brother
before it dropped.

I'm talking an afternoon
like a scratch in an old, favorite record,
the one tooth gnawing
until the thing becomes hateful.

Yeah you,
shirt stuck to your back.

What difference does it make if it's $2 Kesslors
when you're going to throw it up

out behind the filling station,
too drunk for the ball game.

Yeah you,
coupled to this bitch,
one of you running backward

then the other.

I'd like to take this afternoon,
in its burlap sack
barely stirring like a sick, half-grown bluetick
out into the woods and shoot
without aiming.

It'd be a favor to it.

Oh, Lord

cast me hip and thigh
on the spikes of a bad night.

Tear something up, please.

Grease

From bacon, old Fords, makeup,
the fur of the head
and hair of winter mammals,

and for the windows
oozed in paper bags,
the stained glass
where the saints
receive their thorns
and seraphim swarm
like gnats after the fumes
of your incense,

for the way you congeal
and camp in the heart,
the ache of accumulation,
the slick black smoke
of your fires,

for the glistening
on the jowls,
the waxy florets
that bloom
where the warm fat
wiped the plate,

for the way you sour
the stomach of the dog
who has eaten your jelly,
he must eat grass and gag,

for grimy old Tess,
who walks around touching everything
with our fingers,

for you, Brother, you must be tired,
so long on the skids,
so long on the palm,
so long on the wheel,

for the way you must be rendered,
for the way you smear,
for the way you walk on water,

take, drink all of this.

IV

Let My People Go

> Sublime: To transform directly from
> the solid to the gaseous state.

Naphthalene sublimes at room temperature.
The room, for instance, where he said
"Other women, name one,"
the room where she said "No, never"
and shut each cupboard,
the room they brought him into
and did not shut his eyes
and the men outside wiped the sides
of their boots on the grass and waited.
Naphthalene sublimes.

A white crystalline compound, $C_{10}H_8$,
derived from coal tar,
each fossil
steps out onto the normal air
like Jesus hiking over the gunnel,
holding up, just a little, the hem of His robe.

O Naphthalene, I would house like you
in the cedar chest, in the fragrant gate of going away.
I would be useful too,
as a moth repellent, as an explosive.

Naphthalene saves.
I have seen it in neon
and believe those bones.
I have seen the old man dance
the Saint Vitus,
his progress down the street,
his slick hair and worn shoes.

Naphthalene sublimes. Hallelujah.
We are His people, a throng in the noon.
Naphthalene sublimes. Glory be to the Deliverer.
He comes to the gate
and all who go out
will be like the dust of the road,
will rise up.

Jack

I used to do the Alexander Hamilton.
I used to knife that shine,

but after you've cut so many people
thousands of slits like gills

and they still can't breathe,
you get to feeling worn.

I used to rough
and breakdown Friday night,

a pocket crammed with jack
and a mouthful of lies.

I used to love
to put my nickel down.

Now I dance all night
with whoever shows up.

We struggle
to keep each other hugged

all around the room.

Real Jazz

I let my coat do my talking.
It's got a little pocket inside
the inside pocket.

Or you could go the other way
and play the one note of the woman rising
from her pew,
eyes rolled back
the gospel slurring in her blood.

It's easy.
If you want to find
the straight, straight, straight
and narrow,
follow the bat.
He takes it three inches
at a time
and gloves a mosquito
plump on the fever in someone's blood.
He puts hair on the zig-zag.

What mars these American kids,
the horn man says of the good money
loosening at the bar,
is their availability.
His glass is half empty,
his eyes half full,
which, he points out, is how we look
at only half the problem.
*You might have the stop
but somebody else has the door.*

It's the kiss you put on it,
the skitter,

the sugar in the blood
and the way it boils down
with the afternoon
until you get your coat from behind the door
and the empty hanger swings
and keeps the beat
as you walk off down the hall.

Juke

Day Before Killing Day

There are some lucky stuffs
what rise, what break and go from here

without weeping.
Sublime, says the science woman,

who, though she is attracted to me,
is chemical, cording to her,

and will go her own.
You're the nail I tear my shirt on,

I tell her because she goes off
and leave everybody figuring

where she got to.
Sublime, she says like judgment day.

Just gone
and no amount of conjuring

can fetch her back.

I know the incant for hurt foot.
I know the smoke for earache.

She don't preicate me
for my true value, my motions.

Little Walter, I try to explain,
is the president of going on,

playing a Memphis screet
when he was twelve

and the only choice
was sell your ass or make music for change.

But she has her credentials
and they write gone after her name in the book,

cording to her.

That's my surmise, I say,   *Adams?*
the man was first to distort,

first with the dispatcher's mike,
calling down those destinations

that no one could hire,
but only hear tell of.

"I'm going to leave here running
cause walking is most too slow,"

is what he arrive at.
I've got my degrees and am through with lectures

she says to no one in particular
which includes me.

Day before killing day
the day all rats will die.

We must make our preparations,
we must make our solutions,

cording to her who is chief
of the vials and cylinders

though I don't know who made her so.

Chemicals know, she says,
when they shall rise up.

They agitate,
she shakes her foot and smokes.

I'll give her one thing,
she did know

that the breath harp, the Mississippi saxophone,
is the one instrument,

outside us,
that plays both coming and going,

what sings on breathing.

But she's not long for here.
Her finements have a better place

to shake and smoke and ray themselves out,
and leaving is only hard

on what stays behind,
Wednesday, 8:30, empty cages,

new white coat,
day after killing day.

*

Jump

She wondered at the turtle heart I told
and said it wasn't so.

But I said chicken would do it too.
I said snake will crawl back to its hole

if you don't hang it on a fence.

She don't believe.
Her notions wrote down.

"What have you got for proof, besides ignorance?" she says.
"Have you found the graduated cylinders?"

The rats stir when our blood is up
such as it is now.

They sway in their cages.
They smell shake. They hear blood turn.

"Frog leg will jump on its own."
"That's electricity," she says.

My point exactly.

She says the jump is chemical.
I say the jump is spirit.

"Only spirit is in the Adam."
She tries my own line.

But I don't bite.
Conjure always use your own hair.

You catch the old blues man
using his own name in every song.

"Science this," I say.
"We had to straighten the hook with vise grips.

We had to crack the shell with a sledge hammer.
Took a saw to open him.

Took an ax and oak block for his neck.
The kids danced with the stick

and his beak stayed closed.
Women were cleaning the meat.

When we got to the heart,
it still beat."

"Reflex," she says.
"Muscle goes on."

My point exactly.

*

Gone

Corner of Strut and Cobb
on ripped out school bus seats

by trash fires in winter
by flies and stink in summer,

he sits, old emperor of the Watusi
he tell us.

"Your background is too various,"
the science woman says.

Her red, red dress
comes through the white coat.

"I took the mountain cousins to him.
He offered his hand as he always did."

"Rack these in the centrifuge," she says.
She only want what she can count.

She keep two coats.
One for here, one for on the hill.

One for here been caught and burned.
The other is fish-belly, Sunday handkerchief white.

"You had to kiss his hand,
before you got the story."

"But you said there was an accident," she says.
"You said you wasn't listening," I say.

"I'm spinning this down," she counters.
"What else could I do?"

I smile.
"Was the accident you had to kiss.

Anything he wanted to open
he would hold against his body.

He told it the best
behind drinking a little wine.

Him and Fus set out rabbit gums,
little logs with the trap doors.

Quarter a pelt.
Nickel a body on the market.

They were enterprising, cording to him.
They were cat pee and top hat.

Fus pulled the fur off cottontails
like a shirt off his back.

Saved the feet for last.
He ran the chopping block.

Fus ran the ax.

You know Satchmo used to throw
a handkerchief over his hand

so the others wouldn't see
what he was about."

I try to bring her along.
I try to make her various.

"You had to kiss the gone hand.
And you had to do it right."

"Do you believe in anything
you *can* see," she says.

"I believe you listening."

*

Charm

I would meet some conclusion.
"You can draw no conclusion," says the science woman,

"on such evidence."

The science woman scratch her itch
in the green marble notebook.

Somewhere she learn
not to fall for that old breathing

when we beside each other
working on a rack

and the rats start stirring
over head, behind your back,

the rats start swaying
way they do

snake-drunk and willing.
She has her reason, she says.

She take down the changes,
the tabolites.

She speaks in tongues.

She shunt her eyes.
She always safe with her goggles.

"It's an old wives tale," she says.
Sounds right, where I heard it.

"Fear freezes them, not the snake."
What's the difference, I wonder.

He throw a hex.
He stun himself on them.

Evidence is they gone.

"Snake lock hisself
in the hen house

when he swallow an egg
and can't get out the hole

he came in."

"Let it be a lesson to you,"
say the science woman.

She lesson everything.
Gone all the evidence I need.

She the one look in her notebook
for her Adams.

She the one rackin
and countin on her fingers.

Notes

"I'll Fly Away" is for Tom Andrews.

"Photographs from the Mountain Empire" is for Elaine Hall Chitwood and Trobie Washington Chitwood, Jr..

"The Mill" is for the employees of the Angle Plant.

"Juke" is for Bill Newton and Charles Wright.

*

This book was set in Bembo.

*

Michael Chitwood grew up in Redwood, Virginia, in the foothills of the Blue Ridge. His work has appeared in *Threepenny Review, Virginia Quarterly Review, The Ohio Review, Mississippi Review* and other publications. In 1989, he received a fellowship from the North Carolina Arts Council. Nightshade Press published his chapbook, *Martyrdom of the Onions,* in 1991. He lives in Chapel Hill, North Carolina, and makes a living as a science writer.